A Forest for Christmas

A Forest for Christmas

Michael Harris
Illustrations by Eric Orchard

NIMBUS
PUBLISHING

Nimbus Publishing Limited
PO Box 9166
Halifax, NS B3K 5M8
(902) 455-4286

Printed and bound in Singapore

Design: Heather Bryan
Author photo: Lynda Harris
Illustrator photo: Angela Carlsen

Library and Archives Canada Cataloguing in Publication

Harris, Michael, 1948-
A forest for Christmas / by Michael Harris ;
illustrations by Eric Orchard.
ISBN 13: 978-1-55109-589-9   ISBN 10: 1-55109-589-0

1. Christmas stories, Canadian (English). I. Orchard, Eric II. Title.
PS8615.A7479F67 2007   jC813'.6   C2007-901616-2

We acknowledge the financial support of the Government of Canada through the Book Publishing Industry Development Program (BPIDP) and the Canada Council, and of the Province of Nova Scotia through the Department of Tourism, Culture and Heritage for our publishing activities.

For Peyton, Dax and Emily—*MH*

For Julie, with love —*EO*

Emily awakened early, as she always did in the jolly days just before Christmas. She rubbed her eyes and filled her room with a long, musical yawn. Pulling the blankets up to cover her still-sleeping Teddy (he was not a morning bear), she wobbled to the window to see if it had finally snowed.

The pine floor was freezing. Emily hopped from one foot to the other. She opened her curtains but couldn't see through the frosty windowpane. Cupping her hands the way her mama did, she blew gently on the silvery swirls. Magically, a circle appeared. Through it, she could see the village below.

Everything was in its place: the picture-perfect cottages dotting the picture-perfect harbour where fishing boats bobbed at anchor on the twinkling sea. No snow.

Touching the window with her nose, Emily jumped at its icy touch. "The birds must be starving," she said out loud.

Emily pulled on her clothes. She was in such a hurry to get downstairs that she forgot to brush her sleep-tossed hair.

The kitchen was warm and smelled of woodsmoke and shortbread cookies. Everyone chuckled when Emily arrived. Catching her reflection in the gleaming toaster, she could see why. Her hair stood up in the back, straight and stiff.

"Good morning, rooster," her papa teased. Everyone laughed, especially when Emily put her hands on her hips and flapped her arms like wings.

After breakfast, Emily put on her blue coat. It was time to fill the feeders. Usually her mama came along, but not today. There was a meeting at the fire hall—only adults were allowed to go. Emily didn't know why.

Outside, she soon forgot the strange world of grown-ups. Not a single seed was left in the feeder. The birds very much wanted their breakfast. Now, birds' stomachs never growl. But if you listen carefully, as Emily always did, you could sometimes hear them mewing.

The animals were happy to see her.

The squirrels sat on their hind legs and rubbed their paws together.

The chickadees cocked their heads to one side and cheeped.

The blue jays squawked and landed on each other's heads.

The finches poked out of their hiding spots, keeping one eye peeled for the cat.

The pigeons cooed and strutted.

The crows pointed their beaks skyward and cawed uproariously.

High above, a golden eagle circled, making everyone a little nervous.

Emily dipped her wooden scoop into the sack of oiled sunflower seeds by the back door. The chickadees knew what that meant and perched on her hand.

Emily filled the tube-shaped feeder to the brim. Then she hung the red wire basket, with its seed-studded suet ball inside, on a low bough. Before she poured the water, she had to tap her finger to break the see-through pane of ice that had formed in the drinking trough overnight.

Her chores done, Emily lay down in the spruce needles and dreamed of Christmas morning. Gazing up through the thick boughs, she felt snug and happy, which was how the trees always made her feel.

Someone very wise had planted them long ago, before the streets in Lunenburg had names. Now they were the tallest spruce trees in the village and very, very important.

Birds nested in them. Squirrels played tag in them. Bugs burrowed in them. Cats scratched on them. When their big cones fell, each one as long as a kitten's tail, the villagers collected them in wicker baskets to decorate their Christmas wreaths.

Next to her family, this Friendly Forest was the most wonderful thing in Emily's life. She had given each tree a name.

Mr. Big, with his stout branches, kept watch outside her bedroom window.

Squeaky held her wooden swing, creaking whenever she took a ride.

Knocker tapped a delicate limb against the cedar roof to warn when a storm was on the way.

Weepy announced the changes in the seasons with big drops of sap that stuck to her papa's truck like glue.

Lullaby sang her to sleep when the spring breezes jostled the boughs.

But Peek-a-Boo was her favourite. Lunenburg County was the Christmas tree capital of the world, and Peek-a-Boo was the bushiest spruce tree of all. And that was a very good thing. For it was Peek-a-Boo who hid Emily's tree house—and her secret life.

It was in that tree house, just above the woodpecker hole and just below the squirrel's nest, that Emily kept her treasures—an ancient arrowhead, an old pirate coin, and the golden feather of an eagle she had nursed back to health from a broken wing. And, of course, there was the Red Hat.

Emily had found it on the beach one day while she hunted for seashells called silver dollars. It was made of soft felt covered with sequins. It had a broad, droopy brim. Everyone else thought it was only an old hat filled with sand. Emily knew better.

She had first seen the Red Hat one summer night when she was looking at the sky through her telescope. It was perched on the happy, round head of the Man in the Moon. It must have fallen off as he bent down to gaze at his reflection in the ocean. Of all the places in the world, you see, the Moon comes closest to Earth in Lunenburg. As it tumbled to the sea, the Red Hat filled with stardust, which happens to look a lot like beach sand. Stardust, of course, is pure magic.

Deep inside Peek-a-Boo's dense boughs, behind the snug, canvas walls of the tree house, Emily shared her treasures, including the Red Hat, with all of the creatures. In return, the animals taught Emily how to talk to them.

As much as the grown-ups knew (and they knew a lot), none of them had Emily's secret power. It was simple. If you truly love and take care of something, it isn't long before it teaches you its language. And as anyone who regularly talks to animals knows, there is nothing they like more than a good conversation.

Once a week, the creatures in the Friendly Forest flew, crept, climbed, and crawled into the tree house. Cozying down in their favourite spots, they gathered around Emily and shared their news. Emily called it the Story Circle. She served acorns, hummingbird nectar, and wild birdseed so tiny it looked like grains of ebony sand. There was nearly as much to talk about as there was to eat. In spring, the watchful owl told Emily which birds had returned from their winter homes in the south and which ones were overdue. When the leaves came out and the grass turned green, he noted how many eggs had been laid. Later, after they hatched, Owl kept track of which fledglings had learned to fly and which still snuggled in their nest waiting for mama's next worm.

In summer, everyone was too busy raising their babies to say much more than hello. But that didn't stop the squirrels from complaining if the blue jays beat them to the feeder, or if the tourists didn't share their lunches in the picnic-park on Battery Hill.

As the leaves changed colour and fluttered down like red and yellow butterflies, everyone chatted at once in the crowded tree house. Southbound birds said goodbye to the birds that were wintering over. Squirrels and chipmunks talked about the nuts they had stored away. Mole, who could never be too warm, wondered if his burrow had enough leaves and bits of wool to keep him snug in the long, cold nights ahead.

When winter came and icicles hung like sparkling daggers from the eaves of the house, almost no one ventured out except, of course, to get the seeds that Emily left in the big feeder every morning just after sunrise.

In winter, they especially liked to share their dreams with Emily.

The squirrels dreamed of tender shoots.

The robins dreamed of juicy dew worms.

The finches dreamed of sipping rainwater from the cup of a tulip's petals.

Winter, though very beautiful, was much harder for the animals than the warm days of summer. But no one worried. They all knew what to do. If they ran out of food, they tapped twice at Emily's bedroom window. Before they could shake their tails or flap their wings, she would bring nuts and cereal from the pantry.

On the very coldest days, Emily gave her dolls' clothes to the smallest creatures. That way, they stayed warm and cozy, even if the squirrels did make her laugh out loud in their woolen tunics and toques!

In summer and winter and all the getting-there days in between, the spruce trees looked down at the world they sheltered and shook their great, green boughs. That, as Emily knew, is what trees do when they are happy.

The boughs were perfectly still, though, when Emily's parents came back from the meeting later that day. Her papa scarcely touched his bowl of stew. Knitting silently, her mama didn't even laugh when Emily dipped her nose in her milk by mistake. As for Emily's older sister, Peyton, she looked gravely from one parent to the other and didn't say a word. Emily sighed. When things go wrong, the youngest is always the last to find out.

Now, at Christmas, Emily usually dreamed of all the things she loved best: the smell of mincemeat tarts browning in the oven; the familiar carols that filled the house; and most of all, the beautifully decorated tree, with its heap of neatly wrapped presents.

Emily made gifts for her family out of acorns, pinecones, pretty stones, and dried flowers. As Emily's mama always said, not even the Black Duck, a very famous Lunenburg shop, held anything more beautiful. But the mysterious sadness that now hung over the house turned Emily's Christmas world topsy-turvy.

That night she dreamed that her papa's boat, *The Bluebell*, sprouted legs and walked along the wharf. The seagulls wore spectacles and were as green as tropical parrots. The tide went out and never came back. Strangest of all, the stone angel in Mrs. Pittman's back garden walked across the street and knocked on Emily's door: *tap, tap, tap*.

When she opened her eyes, Emily blinked twice to make sure she was awake. *Tap, tap, tap*. The sound got louder and louder. Could that statue really be at the door? she wondered. Her Teddy whispered in her ear, as he often did when she got things wrong. The knocking was coming from her window. Opening her curtains, Emily saw Squirrel. His eyes were wide and very dark, the way they had looked when he was burying an acorn and an oil truck had come too close.

"What is it, Squirrel?"

"Oh Emily!" Squirrel cried, flicking his bushy tail with every word. "Men have come to cut down the trees."

Emily's heart pounded like Rabbit's hind legs thumping on freshly fallen snow. She looked out the window. Squirrel was right. The yard was filled with men. They wore yellow hardhats and big leather gloves. Worst of all, they were carrying chainsaws. The men looked unhappy. You could always tell when people wished they were some place else.

Emily's papa appeared in his checkered woodsman's jacket and rubber boots, and the men gathered around him, speaking in low voices. Emily couldn't hear what they were saying. After a few minutes, they put their saws and red gasoline cans back in their trucks and drove away.

"Good old Papa," Emily cried. "Look Squirrel, he sent the men away."

But when he came back inside, Papa didn't look very happy. It was all Mr. Buggleysmug's fault. Papa explained that Mr. Buggleysmug had come to Lunenburg to make whatzits. Apparently, the town needed a whatzit factory. There were not as many fish as before, but there were just as many people who needed jobs.

Mrs. Buggleysmug liked the town so much she asked her husband to build her a fine house. The couple chose a spot on the hill overlooking the harbour. And that's when the trouble began. The trees around Emily's house were so tall that they spoiled Mrs. Buggleysmug's view. Mr. Buggleysmug told the mayor that unless the trees were cut down, he would build the factory down the shore.

The mayor had called the meeting at the fire hall the day before to pass along Mr. Buggleysmug's warning: no harbour view, no whatzit factory. It made everyone sad, but they had no choice. The trees needed to be cut down.

That's why the men showed up with their saws. But Emily's papa wasn't ready to give up. He convinced the men to let him try one last time to spare the ancient spruce trees.

He went to Mr. Buggleysmug's house. But Mr. Buggleysmug was in a faraway city collecting the money to build his whatzit factory. He wouldn't be flying home until Christmas Eve. Only Mrs. Buggleysmug was home.

"You'd better speak to him yourself," she said sternly when Papa explained what he wanted. She disappeared into the house and returned with Mr. Buggleysmug's telephone number at a city hotel.

Emily's papa phoned Mr. Buggleysmug and pleaded with him to spare the trees. But Mr. Buggleysmug wouldn't listen. Instead, he declared: "In honour of my new factory, you can tell the men to put away their saws…until after Christmas," he added, in his most Buggleysmuggian voice. "But the day after Christmas, the work will begin. Merry Christmas to all, and remember: no harbour view, no factory."

Emily had been listening at the foot of the stairs. "What did he say, Papa?" she asked in a voice a little louder than normal.

"It's no use," came Papa's unusually soft reply. "We can have the trees until Christmas, but the day after that they have to go."

Emily rushed outside and climbed up to the tree house. Every animal in the Friendly Forest was huddled inside, bursting to hear the news.

"They're coming back to cut down the trees," she said sadly. "It's Mr. Buggleysmug's fault."

"Who is Mr. Buggleysmug?" Pigeon wondered.

Emily thought and thought. "The opposite of Santa Claus," she answered.

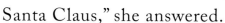

After a long silence, all the animals began to talk at once.

"Where will I build my nest?" Sparrow asked.

"Where will I get my spruce cones?" cried Squirrel.

"How will I sharpen my claws?" Cat chimed in.

"Who will protect us from the storms?" Finch inquired.

And then in one great voice, all the animals shouted: "What will we do without our tree house?"

There was only one thing to do. Emily opened her treasure chest and reached inside. The squirrels wiggled, the sparrows fluttered, and the cat began to purr. They all knew what was coming next.

"The Red Hat," the animals cried. "Put it on," they shouted. "Put on the Red Hat, Emily."

Slowly, she raised the hat high into the air with both hands, looking gravely at each of them. Then, ever so carefully, she lowered it onto her head. Emily's eyes disappeared under the droopy brim and all the animals could see was her chin. A little sand, or rather, stardust, trickled down through her hair. They all held their breath.

18

Emily had only used the Red Hat three times before when they hadn't known what to do: once to find a lost robin's egg, once to help the golden eagle fly again, and the third time was just the other day, to ask for some snow in time for Christmas.

They had found the egg. The eagle had soared. But so far, no snow. Though none of the creatures asked it, the question on all of their minds was this: How could they save the Friendly Forest if the Red Hat couldn't even make it snow?

For a long time, Emily's face remained hidden under the broad, red brim. When she finally took it off, she was wearing a smile so big it made them all smile just to look at her. Smiles, you see, are the only things catchier than colds.

"I know what to do," she cried. "We have to decorate the tallest tree in the Friendly Forest before Mr. Buggleysmug gets home." The creatures understood at once. Not even a man with a whatzit factory could cut down the most beautiful Christmas tree in the world!

That night, after her mama and papa left for the Christmas Eve
dance at the fire hall, Emily and the animals went to work. She took
all the ornaments from the bushy little tree in the family room and
carried them outside in her doll carriage.

In a few moments, the glass balls, wooden bells, and coloured
lights were hanging from Peek-a-Boo's lowest bough. But Emily
could see that they had a big problem. There weren't nearly enough
decorations, goodness no, not nearly enough.

But when Emily had an idea, there was no stopping her. She ran from door to door in the glowing winter dusk, until she had gathered all the children in Lunenburg. Leading them back to the Friendly Forest, she told them that the trees would be cut down unless they could show Mr. Buggleysmug how beautiful they were.

"But we don't have enough ornaments, not nearly enough," she told them, pointing up to Peek-a-Boo's mostly undecorated limbs.

"Don't worry, Emily," they all shouted. "We'll decorate Peek-a-Boo, right to the top."

With that, the children rushed home and gathered all the decorations they could carry. After Mole had carefully pulled out all the plugs, the squirrels climbed onto every rooftop in town and collected string after string of coloured lights. The pigeons and crows ferried them back to the Friendly Forest in their strong beaks. The pile of decorations was soon as large as Farmer Moser's summer haystack at the four corners on the edge of town.

Everyone worked like Santa's elves.

The squirrels wound the lights round and round Peek-a-Boo to the very top.

The blue jays hung the gleaming bulbs higher and higher.

The finches took silver tinsel in their beaks and draped it over every branch.

At last the work was done, except for one thing. Peek-a-Boo had no angel. The angels from the children's trees were too small. Then Owl, who saw everything, spoke to Emily in his wise, owly voice.

"There is a fine, big angel on the *Bluenose II*, just above the crow's nest. I saw a sailor put it up yesterday when I was checking for stale buns behind the bakery."

Although he didn't eat bread himself, Owl knew from past experience that his pigeon friends couldn't get a better Christmas present than a good, day-old croissant from the French bakery.

Emily and her friends hurried down to the harbour. The great ship lay anchored by the wharf. On the very top of its towering mast, as high as the tallest tree in the Friendly Forest, stood the glorious angel. Owl, as usual, was right.

"Hurrah!" the children cried. "It's perfect for Peek-a-Boo."

But how could they get it down? Squirrel climbed up the mast, but the angel was far too big for him. The crows tugged and tugged, but it was far too heavy for them. Even Pfeiffer, the biggest tomcat in town, couldn't budge the angel, though he pushed and pushed with his muscular hindlegs and shoulders.

It was just about then that Emily heard a mighty beating of wings. Everyone looked skyward and gasped.

Something huge and dark hovered over the angel in the winter twilight. It was Eagle, swooping down so effortlessly you would never guess that his wing had ever been broken. Taking the angel in his powerful talons, he lifted it from the schooner's mast and flew away.

When the children got back to the Friendly Forest, there was Peek-a-Boo's angel, perched solidly on the tree's crown. A golden feather drifted to Emily's feet. There was the flapping of distant wings on the winter twilight.

"Thank you, Eagle, wherever you are," Emily shouted into the dark sky. The big moment had arrived.

A hush fell over child and animal alike. Their task was done but what would happen next? The animals slowly turned their gaze to the little girl with the plan. Her heart beating fast, Emily plugged in the tree.

"Ooohhh," they all cried, moving back a step as Peek-a-Boo burst into a dizzying pillar of light and colour. "We did it!" Squirrel cried, dashing up the massive trunk to his favourite limb.

Owl opened his eyes and blinked approvingly.

Pfeiffer gazed up into the glittering boughs and began to purr.

The blue jays twitched, the crows cawed, and the finch, light as a feather, lit on Emily's hand.

"Oh my!" Emily said to them all. "Oh my!"

The children gathered around the great spruce tree and sang O Tannenbaum. Then everyone went home for one last night's sleep before Christmas morning.

Walking back from the dance, the grown-ups didn't know what to think. The whole town was dark. What had happened to all of their Christmas lights? they wondered. When they saw Peek-a-Boo ablaze in the winter night, they scratched their heads. Back in their houses, their own Christmas trees were bare. They scratched their heads again. Things were getting more and more mysterious.

It was just before midnight when Knocker began tapping a warning limb against the cedar roof of the big, old house, the way he always did when a storm was coming. Emily slept and slept.

Outside, whitecaps danced on the harbour and the giant spruce trees swayed in the wind. The snow came, a whole skyful falling in such thick swirls you couldn't see the house next door.

But not everyone was asleep this Christmas Eve.

High above Lunenburg, Mr. Buggleysmug was in trouble. His plane tossed and bumped along like a cork on stormy waters. He looked through the window but all he could see was snow. He didn't like it. He didn't like it one bit.

He tried to give orders, but no one listened. He put on his worst frown, but no one paid any attention. He even counted his money, but it gave him no comfort. They should have seen land by now. If they missed the airport, they would be lost over the ocean. Brrrrh!

Suddenly Mr. Buggleysmug felt the plane descending, rocking to and fro in the howling wind. The faces of the other passengers were pale with fright.

It was at that moment that Mr. Buggleysmug saw it—a dazzling Christmas tree crowned with an angel blazed through the storm-tossed night. Everyone looked out the windows at the magnificent tree and cheered. "That's Lunenburg down there," the pilot cried. "It's a miracle."

"Yes," Mr. Buggleysmug thought aloud, "a miracle to save Cornelius P. Buggleysmug, benefactor to the human race." The builders of whatzit factories often say the strangest things.

Peek-a-Boo's angel guided the airplane out of the clouds, down over the treetops. The plane came to the end of the runway, where it bumped to a stop in a snowdrift taller than Mr. Buggleysmug.

When he finally got back to his fine, new house, he told Mrs. Buggleysmug everything that had happened. When he got to the part about the angel, she took him by the hand and led him to the window overlooking the harbour.

"You mean that angel?" she said, pointing towards Peek-a-Boo and the Friendly Forest.

"Why yes," Mr. Buggleysmug said, full of wonder. "That angel."

On the spot, Mr. Buggleysmug decided that he had never before seen such a beautiful forest. He also declared that harbour view or no harbour view, Lunenburg was the only place for his whatzit factory. Before they went to bed that night, the couple vowed that they would never, ever, allow anyone to cut down the trees in the Friendly Forest. And every year on Christmas Eve, they would help decorate Peek-a-Boo, the magnificent Christmas tree that saved Mr. Buggleysmug's life.

After a perfect Christmas Day in Lunenburg, with the moonlight glistening on the freshly fallen snow, there was a feast just above the woodpecker hole and just below the squirrel's nest. A little girl in a Red Hat served acorns, and hummingbird nectar, and birdseed so tiny it looked like grains of ebony sand.

That night, Squirrel dreamed of tender shoots, Robin dreamed of juicy dew worms, and Finch dreamed of sipping rainwater from the cup of a tulip's petals. Emily dreamed of nothing at all, carried into a deep, velvety sleep by Lullaby's soft song outside her window.

As for the giant spruce trees, they looked down on all that they sheltered and shook their great, green boughs, which, as everyone knows, is what trees do when they are happy.